Red's Nature Adventure

James B. Dworkin
Illustrated by Michael Chelich

ISBN-13: 978-0692079430

ISBN-10: 0692079432

This book is dedicated to the hope that as a young person, you will develop a lifelong interest in learning about the plants, animals and other life forms with which we share this beautiful blue planet.

Through your knowledge and love for the natural world will come a desire to save and protect it for future generations. You can begin your own nature adventure by visiting nature preserves, state and national parks near you.

We wish to acknowledge Shirley Heinze Land Trust, whose mission to preserve natural places and inspire people to appreciate and enjoy nature is the genesis of this book. See the appendix to learn more.

Jim Dworkin and Michael Chelich

On a lovely summer day, Red, the Irish setter, and his friends, Colin and Kenny, go on a hike in the local nature preserve. They have come to see the plants and animals that live here.

1

Suddenly, Red spots a chipmunk on the forest trail, nibbling some seeds. Red is curious and decides to run over and see the chipmunk up close.

The chipmunk is frightened by Red and runs away. Red chases him deep into the woods while Colin and Kenny call for Red to stop.

When Red finally stops running, he is lost. He can no longer hear the boys calling. What should he do now?

After wandering for a while in the forest, Red sees a beautiful Baltimore oriole. Red says, "Excuse me, but I am very thirsty. Can you help me find some water?"

"Yes, of course," the oriole says. "I know where to find water for you to drink. Follow me!" Red follows the oriole on the forest trail as the bird flies high above him.

The oriole leads Red to a gentle forest stream.
Red takes a big drink to quench his thirst.

Sensing that Red is lost, the oriole invites Red
to follow him to his home.

On their way, the oriole tells Red about the other animals whose homes are in the forest.

The two new friends see a pileated woodpecker feeding insects to her chicks. Every year, the woodpeckers raise their young in a cavity in a large tree.

Red spots a wood frog along the edge of the forest stream. Frogs are always on the lookout for insects, slugs, worms and snails to eat.

They also spot some wild turkeys nearby. Turkeys forage for leaves, seeds, fruits, berries, snails, and worms in the woodlands and nearby grasslands.

From the air, the oriole points out a mother coyote who has burrowed a hole in the ground to shelter her pups.

As the two friends walk through the forest,
the oriole tells Red that a forest is a very important
place made up of trees, plants, animals, fungi
and bacteria, that work together to make a special
place called a habitat.

The creatures and plants in this forest habitat
depend on each other and the natural features that
are here in order to live.

When they reach the oriole's home, Red sees the
oriole's beautiful hanging nest and his chicks.
Red would like to visit, but this home is too small,
too high and much too crowded for Red!

Suddenly realizing how hungry he is, Red asks the oriole if he can help him find some food.

The oriole replies, "I do not know what food you like to eat, Red. I will take you to my friend fox, who can probably help you."

The oriole leads Red into an area where
the trees appear to be growing out of the water. The oriole tells
Red that this habitat is called a flatwood forest.

It is here that Red meets the oriole's friend, a red fox. The fox is
very beautiful, and she has the same color fur as Red!

The oriole tells the fox, "My new friend, Red, is very hungry. Can you help him find some food to eat?"

"Yes," the fox replies, "I can take Red to a place where we can find food."

Red says goodbye to the oriole as the fox leads him along a fallen tree trunk that crosses the water-filled landscape.

14

The fox leads Red to a place where a series of
tree-covered ridges rise above narrow wetlands.
The fox tells Red this habitat is called a dune and swale.

Red sees two great blue herons hunting for
frogs and crayfish along the water's edge, as
a red-winged blackbird flies up out of the grass.

Red learns
that dragonflies
hunt for food in
the air and like
to catch and eat
moths, mosquitos,
butterflies,
and even bees!

The fox shows
Red how other
animals in the dune and
swale look for food.

The belted kingfisher
looks for its prey by
hovering above the
water and then diving in
to catch small
fish and crayfish.

They see a snapping turtle lying
just above the water's surface. Snapping turtles
eat plants and also hunt fish, frogs, and reptiles.

The two friends watch as a beaver eats a tree branch. Beavers also eat grasses and clover, wetland plants, tender bark, and young tree shoots.

They build their lodges in the water using branches.

They also see a green heron sitting motionless near the water's edge, waiting for prey to come within striking range. Green herons eat fish, small reptiles, amphibians, and aquatic insects.

While the animals of the dune
and swale like to eat frogs, leaves,
insects and tree branches, Red
has no interest in these foods!

The fox suggests that Red should go to the
nearby prairie for something he
might like.

Red thanks and says goodbye to
his new friend.

As he moves along searching for
food that a dog would like to eat,
a soaring bald eagle searches
for food from high above.

Eventually, Red comes upon a trail in a
sunny place with lots of tall grasses
blowing in the wind.

This must be a prairie, he thinks.

He sees colorful wildflowers,
and in the air above,
spots a monarch butterfly.

Red likes the way the butterfly
floats and flutters overhead,
so he follows along.

Red sees a ruby-throated hummingbird using its straw-like tongue to drink nectar from an obedient plant.

Brown-belted bumblebees nest in the ground and collect pollen to feed their young.

A tiger swallowtail butterfly is drawn to the sweetly scented flowers of the milkweed plant.

In her nest beneath the prairie, a white-tailed field mouse nurses her pups.

After seeing many different animals
and flowering plants, the butterfly turns
down a bend in the winding
trail, where Red is surprised to see
two girls, Abby and Madeline,
enjoying themselves in the shade of
a small group of trees.

Abby is eating a sandwich while
Madeline watches for birds using
a pair of binoculars.

Red sees a goldfinch
flutter out in front of the girls;
but more importantly,
he smells Abby's food!

Red eagerly approaches Abby. She
can see that Red is a very friendly dog.

As hungry as he is, Red politely
sits down in front of her and
stares at the sandwich. This look always
works for him at home!

Abby feeds Red the remaining part
of her sandwich. He is so happy to finally
have something to eat.

Being with the girls reminds him of
Colin and Kenny.

Where are they?

Will he ever find them?

Of course, Colin and Kenny are looking for Red. They call for him, but to no avail. The boys decide to go home and fetch their canoe.

They hope to find Red by paddling down the river and looking for him on both banks.

As for Red, he is tired from all of the walking and running he has been doing.

He is also very hot from being out in the warm sun of the prairie, so he decides to return to the cool forest where he can lie down for a nap.

As Red lowers his head to the ground, he can't help but feel like he is being watched, even though the forest is quiet and peaceful.

When Red awakens from his nap, he is startled
by a big, round face with giant eyes! He jerks his head
up to see a barred owl staring curiously at him.

Red senses that the owl is very wise, so he
tells him that he is looking for his friends Colin and Kenny.

To Red's surprise, the owl abruptly turns and flies away, leaving Red confused as to where he is going. Red decides to follow the owl.

Everything becomes clear when they reach the river's edge and see Colin and Kenny in their boat!

The two boys wave excitedly, calling Red
to their canoe. He runs over
to reunite with his friends.

Red happily jumps into the canoe to rejoin the boys. As they prepare to leave, his friend the oriole appears to see Red off.

What a day, Red thinks.

My new animal friends are very clever. They find their own food and water and build their own homes with the things that are here.

I can't wait to come back again!

THE END

Natural Places Are Important!

As Red learns, the natural places around us are very important for the native plants and animals that need to live there.

The places in this story depict some of the natural communities that we protect in northwestern Indiana.

We invite you to visit these special places!

To find one near you, see the map on the right. Many of our preserves are open to the public from dawn until dusk. There is no entrance fee.

To learn more about Shirley Heinze Land Trust and how we protect these special places, visit **www.heinzetrust.org** and follow us on social media **@heinzetrust**.

Shirley Heinze Land Trust Nature Preserves

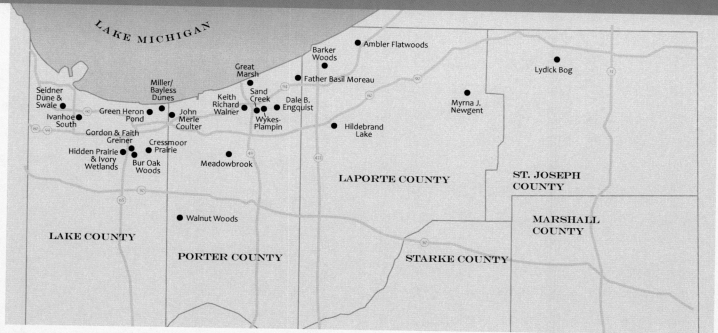

Experience the natural world in northwestern Indiana!

Shirley Heinze Land Trust protects examples of the unique variety of natural communities that are found in northwestern Indiana, including dune and swale, oak savanna, woodlands, prairies, and a variety of wetland ecosystems.

Nature Preserves pictured in the story are listed below with page numbers, along with other preserves where these habitats are found. For more detailed information and directions, please visit heinzetrust.org or call us at 219-242-8558.

Dune and Swale
Seidner Dune & Swale in Hammond *(pp. 15, 16)*
Ivanhoe South in Gary *(p. 19)*

Dunes
Green Heron Pond in Gary
Bayless Dune in Gary
John Merle Coulter in Portage *(pp. 1, 2)*

Prairies
Cressmoor Prairie *(pp. 22, 26, 28),*
and Gordon & Faith Greiner in Hobart

Rivers
Seidner Dune & Swale in Hammond
Wykes-Plampin in Chesterton *(pp. 33, 34, 36)*
Sand Creek in Chesterton
Keith Richard Walner in Porter

Wetlands
Bayless Dune in Gary
John Merle Coulter in Portage
Great Marsh in Beverly Shores
Wykes-Plampin in Chesterton *(pp. 13, 14)*
Lydick Bog in South Bend

Woodlands
Bur Oak Woods in Hobart *(p. 4)*
Walnut Woods in Union Township
Meadowbrook in Valparaiso *(pp. 5, 6, 9, 10)*
Father Basil Moreau in Pine Township
Hildebrand Lake in New Durham Township
Barker Woods in Michigan City *(p. 30)*
Lydick Bog in South Bend

Flatwood Forest
Ambler Flatwoods in Michigan City *(p. 12, 32)*

What Is a Nature Preserve?

A nature preserve is land kept in its natural state in order to safeguard its physical features, and the plants and animals that live there.

As precious natural land is increasingly lost to human activity, protecting, restoring, and re-connecting this habitat for native plants and wild animals is critical for their survival.

Why do people need nature?

Human beings are part of the natural world, just like animals and plants. The air we breathe, the water we drink, and the food we eat all depend on a healthy natural world.

People need natural places, too. It's good for us to get outside to experience these special places and learn about the other living things that need them.

What is a land trust?

A land trust is a charitable organization that works to permanently conserve natural land. We own and care for our nature preserves in the *public trust,* which means **for the benefit of the public**. Shirley Heinze Land Trust accomplishes this work through a partnership of volunteers, donors, and professionals.

Who was Shirley Heinze?

Shirley Heinze Land Trust was named in honor of a woman who cared deeply about the special natural places that are found throughout northwestern Indiana. Two people, Robert and Bette Lou Seidner, wanted to honor the memory of their good friend, Shirley. In 1981, they donated money to start an organization that would work to protect these places forever.

What You Can Do

Connect with Nature

Visiting a nature preserve is a little different than going to a park, with man-made playgrounds and lawns. In a nature preserve, you can enjoy hiking, running, and skiing on trails, and in some preserves, kayaking and canoeing, however; the most important experience is appreciating the natural landscape and the plants and animals that need these natural places in which to survive.

To fully connect with nature, use all of your senses. Feel the physical contours of the land by walking on earthen trails. Listen to the sound of leaves and grasses rustling in the wind, and the songs of birds, and buzzing insects. Inhale the fresh, cool air of woodlands and the scent of wildflowers. Look carefully to see the living things along the trail. If you have them, bring binoculars, and a magnifying glass.

Many of our preserves are located within or near cities, where you can easily visit and enjoy the wild beauty of nature, and understand how important it is for us not to lose such precious natural places.

Get Involved

You can help us protect and care for these precious places. Begin by learning more about the natural world around us. Attend guided hikes and workshops. Visit our website, www.heinzetrust.org, sign up for newsletters, and follow us on social media @heinzetrust.

Shirley Heinze Land Trust
109 West 700 North
Valparaiso, IN 46385
219-242-8558
www.heinzetrust.org

Volunteer your time to walk the trails and pick up litter, or attend a volunteer workday, where you can work alongside our professional stewardship staff.

Share your talents. There are a variety of committees that coordinate the work we do. Let us know if you would like to volunteer your professional or personal services.

And finally, if you can, please support our work with a monetary contribution, or by attending our fundraising events.

Thank you!

James B. Dworkin, an Indiana-based educator, is chancellor emeritus at Purdue University North Central and a professor of management at the Krannert Graduate School at Purdue University. He is the author of two academic books and has published more than eighty articles on labor economics and labor relations. Red's Nature Adventure is his third children's book.

Michael Chelich is a fine artist/illustrator in Munster, Indiana. He paints a variety of subject matter, including portraits, narrative figurative artwork, still life, wildlife, and landscapes. Mike's artwork has been published in several national art magazines including American Artist and The Artist's Magazine.

The artist would like to thank the staff of the ornithology department at the Field Museum for their assistance, and is grateful to Neal and Diane for allowing their Irish setter to be the model for Red.

See more of his artwork at michaelchelich.com

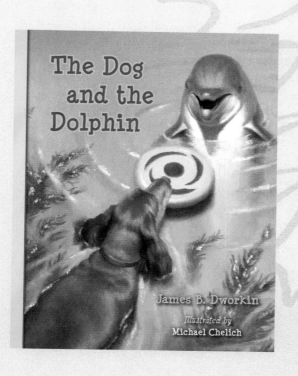

Readers who have enjoyed Red's Nature Adventure will also enjoy Jim and Mike's first two books, The Dog and the Dolphin and The Dog and the Jet Ski. To order your copy of these fun books, visit Amazon.com. To watch for new books, follow @thedogandthedolphin on Facebook.

Made in the USA
Middletown, DE
28 December 2019